The Neighborhood Surprise

Sarah van Dongen

For all my lovely neighbors.
Sarah van Dongen

Copyright © Tiny Owl Publishing 2021
Text and illustrations © Sarah van Dongen 2021

Sarah van Dongen has asserted her right under the Copyright, Designs and
Patents Act 1988 to be identified as Author and Illustrator of this work.

First published in the UK and US in 2021 by Tiny Owl Publishing, London.
With special thanks to Knights Of Publishers for their support.

For teacher resources and more information, visit
www.tinyowl.co.uk
#NeighbourhoodSurprise

A catalogue record for this book is available from the British Library.
A CIP record for this book is available from the Library of Congress.

UK ISBN 978-1-910328-70-5
US ISBN 978-1-910328-71-2

Printed in China

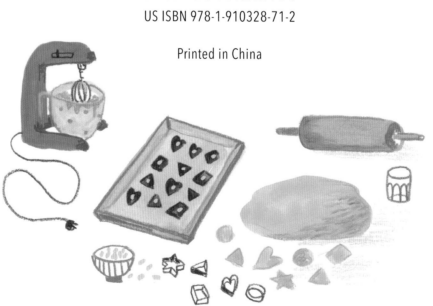

The Neighborhood Surprise

Sarah van Dongen

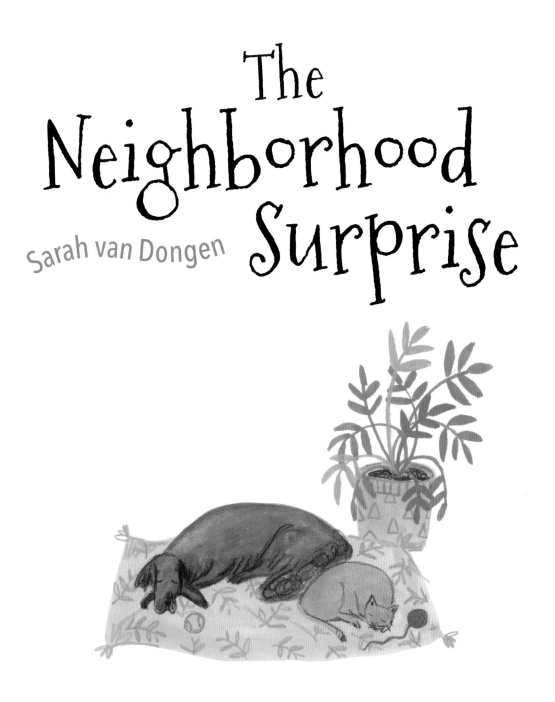

TINY OWL

This is Redbird Road.
Koya lives here,
not far from Mrs. Fig.

Koya and her friends, Hassan and Alex,
love to visit Mrs. Fig.

Mrs. Fig tells the children exciting
stories from the past ...

... she stitches together amazing
costumes for them to dress up in ...

... she has the cutest pets to cuddle ...

... and, best of all, she bakes
the most delicious cookies.

But one day, Dad tells Koya and her friends that Mrs. Fig is moving away.

They are very upset. They will miss their friend.

"Let's organize a going away party!" says Koya.

"That's a good idea!" says Dad.
"The whole street can help."

Koya and her dad want
to bake a cake.

"Hassan is vegan," says Koya. "Can we make it a vegan cake so he can eat it, too?"

Hassan and his mom
make falafel and
a spicy curry.

"Alex thinks your curries are amazing, Mom," says Hassan.

Alex and her family work together to make a pie.

"Mrs. Fig is vegetarian, so it must be a vegetable pie," says Alex.

Soon, everyone in the neighborhood is cooking and baking.
There is lots to do!

On the day of the party, it is a sunny afternoon.
The whole neighborhood brings out tables and chairs.

Koya, Hassan, and Alex knock on Mrs. Fig's door.

"Hello, dears!" smiles Mrs. Fig.

Then she looks out onto the street.

"Oh my..."

"SURPRISE!" yells Hassan.

"We're having a goodbye party for you!" says Koya.
"The whole neighborhood is here."

What a party it is!
"It all looks delicious," says Mrs. Fig.

"Look, I made this pie," says Alex.
"It's vegetarian, just like you!"

"And I made a vegan cake," says Koya.

"This has been wonderful, dears,"
says Mrs. Fig. "But, you know, I'm only moving
to the retirement home across the street..."

"Then we must have a party next year, too!"
says Koya. "Will you promise to make some
cookies for it, Mrs. Fig?"

"Of course, I will," laughs Mrs. Fig.
"As long as you promise to visit me
in my new home!"

Hello! I'm Sarah and I'm an illustrator. I like plants, dogs, and cakes. In this story some people were vegan and some vegetarian. Do you know what these words mean?

When someone is a vegetarian it means they don't eat meat or fish.

When someone is vegan it means that they don't use anything from animals. So they don't eat or drink milk or butter, or honey or eggs or meat or fish. They don't wear wool or leather either, because these come from sheep and cows.

Why would someone be vegan or vegetarian?

It can be because they love animals too much to hurt them.

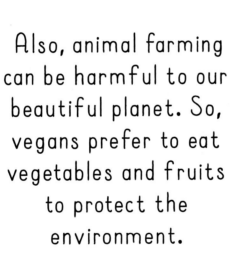

Also, animal farming can be harmful to our beautiful planet. So, vegans prefer to eat vegetables and fruits to protect the environment.